GRANDMAS
AT THE LAKE

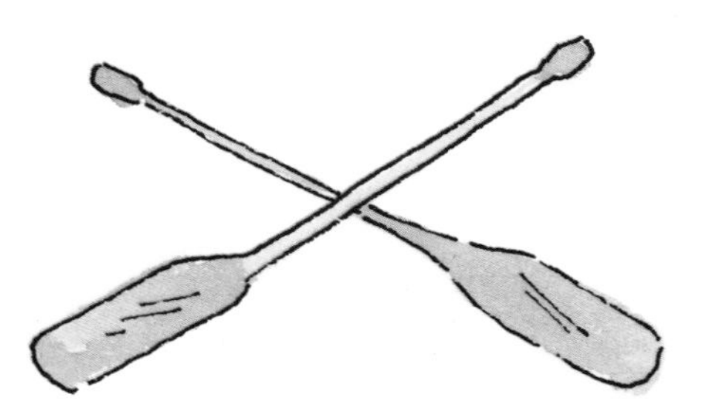

An I Can Read Book®

GRANDMAS AT THE LAKE

story and pictures by

Emily Arnold McCully

HarperTrophy®
A Division of HarperCollinsPublishers

Printed in the United States of America. For information address
HarperCollins Children's Books, a division of HarperCollins Publishers,
10 East 53rd Street, New York, NY 10022.

Library of Congress Cataloging-in-Publication Data
McCully, Emily Arnold.
Grandmas at the lake : stories and pictures / by Emily Arnold McCully.
p. cm. —(An I can read book)
Summary: Pip and Ski have a hard time enjoying themselves at the lake with Pip's two grandmothers, who cannot agree on anything.
ISBN 0-06-024126-8. — ISBN 0-06-024127-6 (lib. bdg.)
ISBN 0-06-444177-6 (pbk.)
[1.Grandmothers—Fiction. 2. Lakes—Fiction.] I. Title. II. Series.
PZ7.M13913Gr 1990 89-36590
[E]—dc20 CIP
AC

First Harper Trophy edition, 1994.

For Raya, and B.G.,

and three generations of sailors

One hot summer day

Grandma Nan telephoned.

"I have rented a cabin at the lake,"

she said.

"I have invited Grandma Sal.

We would like Pip to visit too."

Grandma Sal said,

"Tell Pip to bring a friend.

The more the merrier."

"Tell them to be good,"

said Grandma Nan.

"Oh, Nan," said Grandma Sal.

Pip asked Ski to come along.

"We can swim and hike and row,

and have a great time!" said Pip.

"I can't wait!" said Ski.

When they got to the lake,
Ski shouted, "Last one in
is a rotten egg!"

“Hold on there,”

said Grandma Nan.

“First you unpack.”

"Throw your stuff anyplace,"

said Grandma Sal.

"Not so fast," said Grandma Nan.
"Underwear goes in this drawer.
Shirts and shorts go in this one."

"Whatever," said Grandma Sal.

“Now may we swim?” asked Pip.

“Why not?” said Grandma Sal.

“First we eat lunch,”

said Grandma Nan.

“Then we wait one hour.

Then we swim.”

Grandma Nan made
tuna and sprout sandwiches.
Grandma Sal opened a bag of cookies.
"No cookies
until you eat your sandwiches,"
said Grandma Nan.
"What's the difference?"
said Grandma Sal.
"They will end up together anyway."

Everyone waited exactly one hour.

Then Pip and Ski put on

their bathing suits.

So did Grandma Nan.

“Oh, no,” said Ski.

“Is she coming too?”

“Dip time!” called Grandma Sal.

“Oh, no,” said Ski.

"Stay inside the ropes,"
said Grandma Nan.
"No splashing!"
"Relax, Nan," said Grandma Sal.
"It's only water."

Pip and Ski dove.

"Where are the children?"

cried Grandma Nan.

She blew and blew her whistle.

Pip and Ski came up for air.

"Take it easy, Nan,"

said Grandma Sal.

"You have upset the fish."

Grandma Nan swam ten laps.

Then she blew her whistle again.

“Time to dry off!” she called.

“But we are not ready!” said Pip.

“You do not want to catch a chill,”

said Grandma Nan.

“A chill?” said Grandma Sal.

“The sun is hot as blazes!”

Grandma Nan led them back
to the cabin.
"Pip," said Ski, "these grandmas
will drive me nuts.
If one says yes,
the other says no."
"Let's get away from them,"
said Pip.
"How about playing in the woods?"
"Right!" said Ski.
"Let's go play in the woods!"

"Ski and I are going for a walk,"
said Pip.
"Great!" said Grandma Nan.
"We will take a nature hike."
"But we want to be alone!" said Pip.

"Nonsense!" said Grandma Nan.

"You cannot have fun alone!"

said Grandma Sal.

"We will write down what we see

in this nature notebook,"

said Grandma Nan.

"How about cookies for the hike?"
asked Grandma Sal.

"No. Dried fruit and sunflower seeds
are good for a hike,"
said Grandma Nan.

“Oh, no,” said Pip.

“Our plan has failed.”

“We have to think of another one,”

said Ski.

They followed a path into the woods.

"Hark!" said Grandma Nan.

"Is that the song

of the tufted titmouse?"

"Search me," said Grandma Sal.

"Let's sing along, kids.

Merrily we roll along, roll along..."

"You have scared away the titmouse,"

said Grandma Nan.

"Let's have our snacks,"

said Grandma Sal.

Grandma Nan got out the dried fruit

and sunflower seeds.

"This is for the birds,"

said Grandma Sal.

"Good idea," said Grandma Nan.

"We will feed the birds."

Pip and Ski scattered some seeds.

"We will never have any fun,"

said Ski.

"We will think of a way," said Pip.

"Let us clean up our campsite,"

said Grandma Nan.

"It is time to go home."

“Who wants a nap?”

asked Grandma Sal.

She plopped down on her bed.

Grandma Nan yawned.

“I am worn out,” she said.

“Lie down, Pip and Ski,” she said.

Soon the grandmas were asleep.
Pip and Ski heard them snore.
"This is our chance!" said Pip.
"Let's go!" said Ski.

They tiptoed to the door.

Slowly, they opened it.

Creak, creak.

"Where to?" asked Ski.

"To the middle of the lake!" said Pip.

"They can't bother us there!"

"Grandma Nan might get mad,"

said Ski.

"Grandma Sal would want

to come too,"

said Pip.

Just then they heard
"YOO-HOO!"

"Oh, no," said Pip.

"Here they come!"

Pip untied the boat.

Ski jumped in and sat down.

Pip jumped in and shoved off.

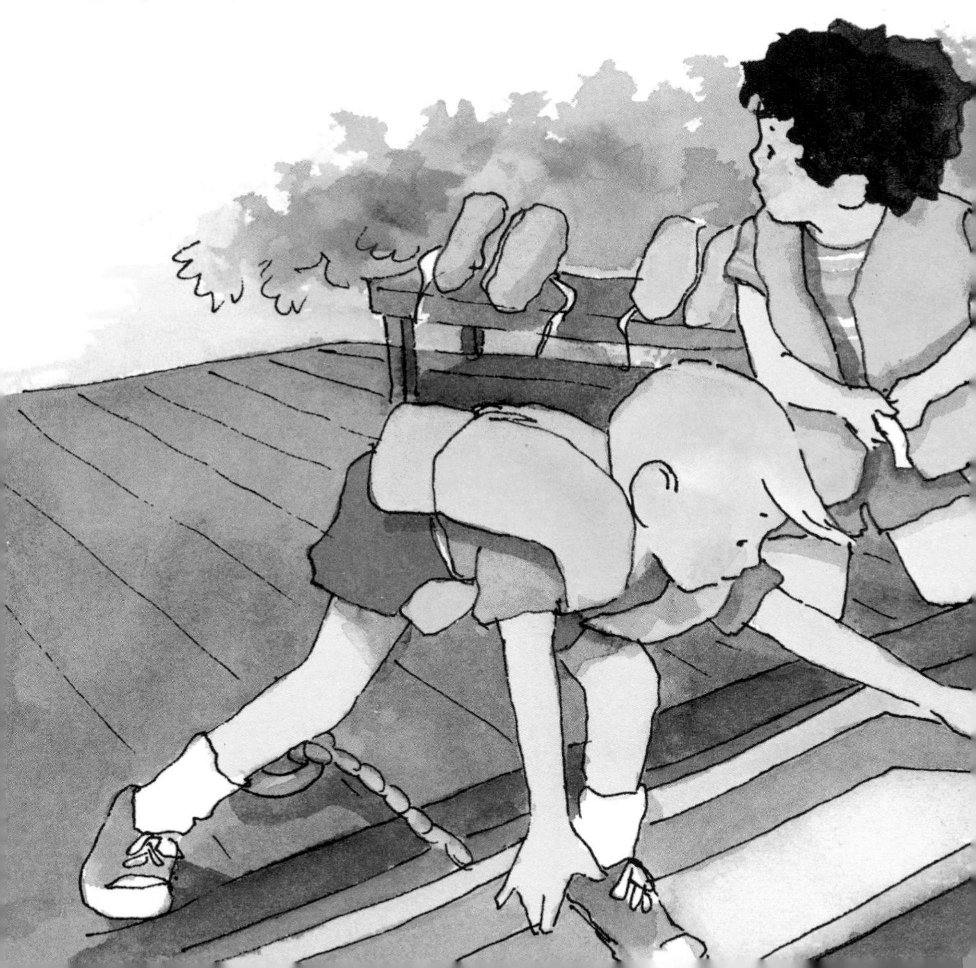

"EEEEEK!" cried Grandma Nan.

"Come back, come back!"

"We are just taking
a little ride," said Pip.

Pip and Ski watched Grandma Nan get smaller and smaller.

Grandma Sal ran to the dock.

“Pip and Ski are lost at sea!”

cried Grandma Nan.

“How could they leave

without us?” said Grandma Sal.

The boat turned in circles.

"We have to row together," said Pip.

They tried again.

The boat moved in a straight line.
Grandma Nan and Grandma Sal
got even smaller.

"This all happened
because I took a nap!"
cried Grandma Nan.
A crowd gathered on the dock.
Everyone waved at the boat.
"Those kids are good sailors,"
said Grandma Sal.
"And they are wearing
their life preservers."

"Let's row to that island," said Pip.

"Okay," said Ski.

"We had better go back now," said Pip.

"The grandmas will be worried."

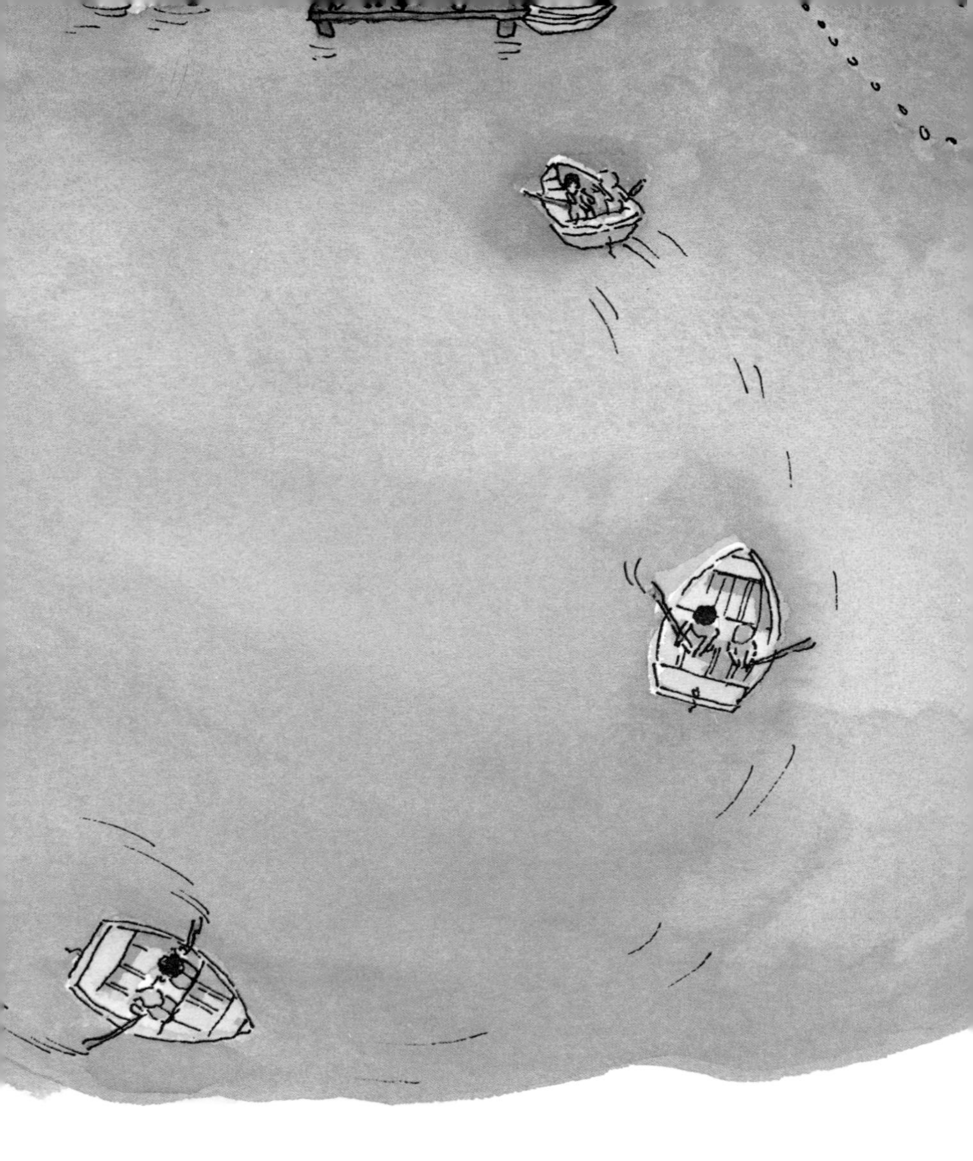

They rowed and rowed
toward the dock.

"Pip! Ski!" called Grandma Nan.

"Please come back!"

"We will if you make us a promise,"

said Pip.

"What do you mean?"

asked Grandma Nan.

Pip said,

"I mean Grandma Nan says one thing

and Grandma Sal says another.

You never let us say what we want."

"Pip has a point," said Grandma Sal.
"What do you want us to promise?"

"Promise to let us have fun!" said Pip.
"Promise to let us play
by ourselves," said Ski.

“Sal?” asked Grandma Nan.

“Okay by me,” said Grandma Sal.

“We promise!” called the grandmas.

"Thank you!" said Pip and Ski.

They rowed up to the dock.

"Will you come for a ride?"

asked Pip.

"Well," said Grandma Nan.

"We would love to!"

said Grandma Sal.

Grandma Nan sat in the stern.

Grandma Sal sat in the bow.

Pip and Ski rowed back

to the middle of the lake.

"Kids," said Grandma Sal,

"you run a tight ship!"

"Relax and enjoy the ride," said Ski.

They rowed past the island.

"This is very nice,"

said Grandma Nan.

"But Ski needs to pull more

on his oar."

"Don't rock the boat, Nan,"

said Grandma Sal.